This book is a work of fiction. Any references to historical events, real people, or real places are used fictitiously. Other names, characters, places, and events are products of the author's imagination, and any resemblance to actual events or places or persons, living or dead, is entirely coincidental.

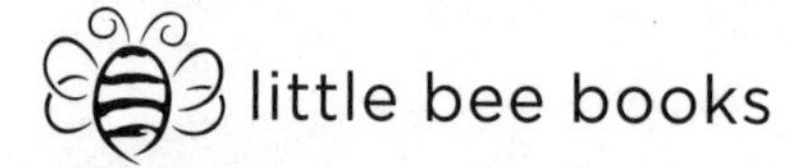

An imprint of Bonnier Publishing USA
251 Park Avenue South, New York, NY 10010

Manufactured in China TPL 0618
ISBN: 978-1-4998-0607-6 (hc)
First Edition 10 9 8 7 6 5 4 3 2 1
ISBN: 978-1-4998-0606-9 (pbk)
First Edition 10 9 8 7 6 5 4 3 2 1

Library of Congress Cataloging-in-Publication Data
is available upon request.

littlebeebooks.com
bonnierpublishingusa.com

Tales of SASHA

The Disappearing History

by Alexa Pearl

illustrated by Paco Sordo

little bee books

Contents

CHAPTER 1 A Royal Horse

"Come out, come out, wherever you fly!" called Kimani.

Sasha ducked behind a cloud. It was big and heavy with raindrops. She flapped her wings, hovering in place. She stayed very quiet.

Does Kimani see me? wondered Sasha.

No! Her friend Kimani flew right by.

Sasha still didn't move. The twins, Marigold and Sonali, were playing hide-and-seek too. Sasha searched the sky. She didn't see them anywhere.

Suddenly, Marigold zoomed up behind her. She reached out her hoof and tagged Sasha. "I found you!"

"Where did you come from?" cried Sasha.

Marigold pointed to another cloud below. "There's a horse behind every cloud!"

Playing hide-and-seek with flying horses on a cloudy day was tricky!

"My turn to hide." Marigold's bright-yellow body streaked away across the sky.

Kimani darted after Marigold to look for a hiding spot as well. Her violet feathers flapped fast.

Sasha took off too. The wind rushed across her face and ruffled her gray mane. She loved flying at a fast speed.

"Whoa!" cried Sasha as the Toucan suddenly flew in front of her.

"Toodle-loo! Sapphire wants to see you!" he called.

"Right after I find Marigold." Sasha didn't want to stop playing the game.

"Oh, no, no, no," said the Toucan. "Sapphire means right now!"

Sapphire was in charge of the flying horses that lived in Crystal Cove and the Toucan was her messenger. So everyone did what Sapphire asked—including Sasha.

Sasha followed the Toucan down to the Crystal Cove beach. The sand sparkled with jewels and gems. The flying horses lived inside caves carved into the rocky cliff. But instead of leading Sasha to the golden door of Sapphire's home, the Toucan brought her to a red door.

"Where are we?" Sasha had never been inside this cave.

"The Royal Library," said the Toucan. "Important books and maps are kept here." He tapped the door five times with the tip of his beak.

Sapphire opened the door. "Welcome, Princess!" Sapphire's wing feathers shined deep blue. Sapphire was one of the oldest horses in Crystal Cove.

"Oh, please, Sapphire. You should call me Sasha." Sasha rocked back on her hooves. "Princess sounds so . . . serious."

"Being the Lost Princess is serious," said Sapphire. "Important too."

"Yes, I know." It felt so strange to be the Lost Princess of the flying horses. Up until a little while ago, Sasha hadn't known she was a flying horse. Sometimes she still couldn't believe that she could fly.

Sasha stepped into the Royal Library and gasped. "It's so beautiful."

Shelves reached from the floor to the ceiling as far as she could see. They were filled with hundreds of books in all the colors of the rainbow and ancient-looking, rolled-up scrolls. Huge maps decorated the ceiling. Sasha stared in wonder.

"I've called you here for this." Sapphire led her to a golden table in the middle of the library. A thick scroll lay on it. "This contains the history of the flying horses." She unrolled the scroll. It was made of enchanted fabric. The long tapestry spilled over the side of the table and across the floor. "It's time for you to read these old stories. As a royal horse, they must become part of you."

"Part of me? All of them?" Sasha stared in horror. The fabric seemed to go on forever.

"Yes. You will pick your favorite and read it to the flying horses on History Day."

"When is that?" asked Sasha.

"Tomorrow," said Sapphire.

Sasha gulped. She could never read all those words so fast!

Sapphire rolled up the fabric. "Be very careful. It is our only written record. Before you go to sleep for the night, bring the fabric back here. Put it on this special golden table to keep it safe. Do you understand?"

"Yes," promised Sasha. She stared at the door, wanting to rejoin the game.

Can I go back to my friends now? she wondered.

"Learn the stories, Princess," said Sapphire, as if reading her mind. "They are important to our herd. You are a royal horse with a royal job to do."

Sasha turned her gaze away from the door. "I won't let you down."

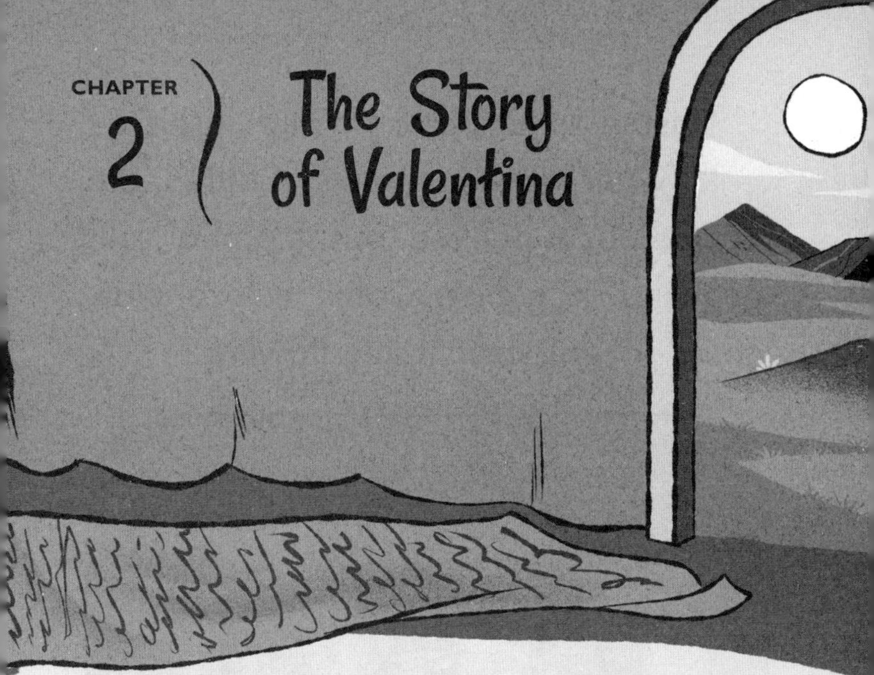

CHAPTER 2

The Story of Valentina

Sasha settled down on some fluffy pillows. Kimani's cave was decorated with brightly patterned blankets and large, cozy pillows. She and Kimani shared a platter of sunflowers and carrot cake for dinner. Sasha had been reading the fabric all afternoon in Kimani's cave.

Outside, the sky grew dark and the moon rose.

"Listen to this story," said Sasha.

"I want to hear too!" Collie's tiny purple face peeked out from a tulip growing in a pot. Collie was a plant pixie, so she slept inside flowers.

"Sure. Have a seat." Sasha waited until her small friend was settled on top of the petals. Then she began to read.

"Long ago, before the stars became stars, an evil dragon named Volcano ruled the sky. He soared from one end of the rainbow to the other, breathing fire wherever he went. The air grew thick with smoke. Ash rained down from the clouds. Soot coated the wings of the flying horses. They fell from the sky, unable to fly."

Kimani gasped. "What happened to them?"

"The horses were stranded on an island. The dragon shot flames out of his mouth whenever they tried to fly. As the horses couldn't swim, they were trapped. Everyone was afraid of the dragon . . . everyone except Valentina."

"Who was that?" Collie asked Sasha.

"Valentina was the smallest horse on the island," read Sasha. "She was a royal horse."

“Oh, I like her. She’s small like me.” Collie tucked her hair behind her pointy ears and leaned in.

“And royal like me.” Sasha began to read again. “Valentina flew up to the rainbow to stop the dragon.”

“How? Didn’t the soot clog her wing feathers?” asked Kimani.

"Valentina called to four large spiders that lived in the island trees. She told them her plan. They spun webs around her wings. The webs were loose enough to let her fly, but they kept the ash and soot off her feathers."

Collie clapped her hands. "So smart!"

"Valentina flew to the rainbow. The dragon blew fire, but the webs kept her wings safe. Then came the big surprise! Hundreds of spiders crawled out of her mane. Quickly, they spun webs around and around the dragon. The webs were made of the strongest silk. Soon, the dragon couldn't move."

Collie nodded. "Then what?"

"Valentina carried the bound dragon to the top of the highest mountain. She put him in a big hole," Sasha went on.

"What about the horses?" asked Kimani. She yawned and snuggled into the blankets.

"The horses flew free." Sasha yawned too. It was getting late.

"Is the dragon still up on that mountain?" asked Collie.

"He is. You can tell when Volcano the dragon is upset, because he spits fire out of the mountaintop," said Sasha.

“Valentina saved the flying horses.” Collie sighed. “What a great story. Read another. Please!”

“Shhh.” Sasha pointed. Kimani had already fallen asleep. “Tomorrow.”

“But—” started Collie.

Sasha’s eyelids grew heavy. Just before she closed them, she remembered the special golden table in Sapphire’s cave.

I’ll bring the fabric back in the morning, she decided. She tucked it close to her body. *It’ll stay safe with me.*

CHAPTER 3 Where Are the Words?

Sasha woke early the next morning. She kept her eyes closed and listened to the sounds of Crystal Cove: the flapping of wings as horses took to the sky, the *thwap-thwap* of the jump ropes as rabbits played double Dutch in the field, the shrill cries of peacocks.

"'Morning," whispered Kimani.

Sasha opened her eyes. "Hi."

"I fell asleep while you were reading last night." Kimani stood and stretched.

"I know. It was a pretty good story, wasn't it?"

"Totally. Collie! Hey, Col? Want to go find some breakfast?" called Kimani.

Collie didn't answer.

They both looked over at the tulip. Its petals were wide open. Collie wasn't inside.

"She must be off doing plant pixie things," said Sasha. Plant pixies made sure the fields stayed green and healthy.

"Do you want to get breakfast with me?" asked Kimani. "The daisies are blooming in the meadow."

Sasha reached for the rolled-up fabric tucked beside her. "I need to bring this back to the Royal Library. I was supposed to last night but . . ." Her voice trailed off. She hadn't kept her promise.

"Read one more story first. Then we can return it together," said Kimani.

Sasha agreed. She unrolled the enchanted fabric. Her eyes went wide. "What happened?"

Kimani scooted closer. “Where are the words?”

The two horses stared at the tapestry. It was completely blank! All the words were gone.

Sasha shook the fabric out. She turned it around. She rolled it up and unrolled it again. The stories were still nowhere to be seen.

"The history of the flying horses has been erased!" she cried.

"How could that be?" asked Kimani.

"I don't know." Sasha chewed her lip nervously. "Do you think it's because I didn't put it back last night?"

"Maybe," said Kimani.

Sasha groaned. Her stomach twisted. This was bad.

"Toodle-loo! Good morning!" The Toucan poked his beak into the cave.

"Sapphire wants to see you in her cave, Princess."

Kimani stepped forward. She blocked the Toucan from seeing that they still had the fabric. "When?"

“Now,” said the Toucan.

Sasha groaned again. This was *very* bad.

CHAPTER 4 Lavender Honey

"I'll be right there." Sasha tried to keep her voice steady.

The Toucan left to let Sapphire know the Lost Princess was on her way.

Sasha's heart beat quickly. Her breath came fast. "Do you think she knows I didn't put the fabric back in the special place? Do you think she knows that the words disappeared?"

"Maybe not." Kimani didn't sound too sure. "She might not have visited the Royal Library today."

"But maybe yes. What should I do?"

"You could tell her the truth."

"I can't. I haven't proven myself to be a good princess yet. She'll never trust me now." Sasha lay down and pulled the blanket over her head. She felt sick.

"Hello?" The Toucan was back. "Ready yet? Please pick up the pace."

"Why does Sapphire want to see her?" Kimani asked the Toucan, not letting him into the cave.

"To plan History Day," said the Toucan.

"That's it?" asked Kimani. "Nothing else?"

"Yes. What's with all the questions? History Day is today, you know. Therefore you must hurry, hurry!"

It sounded to Sasha as if Sapphire didn't know about the missing stories. At least not yet.

The Toucan peered around Kimani. “Why is Sasha under that blanket?”

“I have a bellyache.” Sasha’s voice came out muffled.

“Give her a spoonful of lavender honey,” the Toucan told Kimani. He pointed to a small ceramic pot of honey Kimani kept on a shelf. “It will help settle her belly. When she feels better, send her to Sapphire.”

"Will do! Honey, it is. Thank you!" Kimani shooed him away.

Sasha waited a few minutes then pushed back the blanket.

"That was smart to fib to get him to go away," said Kimani.

"I didn't fib," said Sasha. "Just thinking about what I did and telling Sapphire does make my belly hurt." She took a lick of honey.

"What if we can get the words back and fix the fabric before you see Sapphire?" suggested Kimani.

Sasha perked up. "That's a great idea!"

CHAPTER 5

The Great Escape

"What's your plan?" asked Sasha.

"My plan? I don't have any plan," said Kimani. "I don't know how to get the words back."

"Me neither." Tears pricked the corners of Sasha's eyes.

"Please don't cry." Kimani nuzzled her friend. "Don't worry, we'll find someone to help us. How about Xanthos? He runs the flying horse council."

"Xanthos is all about following the rules. He won't understand," said Sasha.

"How about Crimson? She helped you pass the Princess Test," suggested Kimani.

Sasha shook her head. "Crimson might tell Sapphire."

"Pretty much all the flying horses will tell Sapphire," said Kimani. "We need a horse who can't fly, but who is very smart and believes in magic."

"We need Caleb!" cried Sasha.

Caleb had been Sasha's teacher. He lived with the non-flying horses in Verdant Valley. He'd sent her to Sapphire when her wings first popped out. He was very old and very wise.

"Let's go to Verdant Valley right now," said Sasha.

Kimani peeked out the cave door. Colorful horses exercised in a row on the beach. The Toucan waited nearby. "Big problem. We'll be seen if we fly off to find Caleb. You're supposed to be sick, remember?"

"Where's Collie? She can go to Verdant Valley and talk to Caleb for me." Sasha whistled her special whistle.

She waited. She whistled again.

No Collie.

That's strange, she thought. Collie always came when she whistled. Collie could hear the special sound miles away.

"She'll be back soon," said Kimani. Collie was never far off.

"We can't wait," said Sasha. Time was running out. The Toucan would return. "We need to sneak out without anyone seeing us somehow."

A sly smile spread across Kimani's lips. "I used to sneak out to eat berries when I was little."

"Great! Show me what to do." Sasha tucked the fabric history inside a backpack. She added the pot of lavender honey too and then strapped the backpack onto her back.

Kimani pulled two huge monstera leaves from under a blanket. They were shaped like enormous fans. She gave one to Sasha. "Hold the stem between your teeth and turn it just so. Like that, you can cover your body with the leaf."

Sasha did as Kimani suggested, but her backside still poked out. She swished her tail. "It doesn't cover all of me."

"Just move quickly, like you're a tree."

"That's silly!" said Sasha. "Trees don't move."

"Our trees do."

Kimani watched the horses exercise on the beach.

Squat. Bend. Lift. Stretch.

"Go!" she told Sasha.

The horses had stretched their wings wide. Rows and rows of feathers blocked the sight of two moving palm leaves—and Sasha and Kimani hidden behind them.

They made it out of the cave and into the jungle.

CHAPTER 6 All Eyes on Me

Sasha and Kimani hurried across the jungle. They came out at the end of the beach—far away from the Toucan.

Nearby, a peacock stood guard. “Eye see you!”

“No, you don’t.” Kimani covered her face with the palm leaf.

"In fact, all my eyes see you." The peacock's beautiful feathers had a black circle on the end of each one that looked like an eye.

"It's not me they see," said Kimani. "I'm a tree."

The peacock tilted his head.

Sasha waved her tail. "It's time to make like a tree and leaf."

Sasha and Kimani ran past him.

They ran past spider monkeys on scooters.

They ran past flamingoes twirling Hula-Hoops.

They ran past hedgehogs playing hopscotch.

They didn't dare slow down. Once the Toucan realized they were missing, he'd sound an alarm.

Sasha and Kimani reached the lake. The ferry was waiting, and they stepped on board.

The beaver captain had his sailor's cap over his eyes. He was fast asleep.

"Hurry! Let's go!" Kimani gave him a poke.

"It's not time. The ferry schedule says so," the beaver said sleepily.

"When is it time?" asked Sasha.

"When I see my reflection in the lake below." The beaver yawned.

Sasha peered over the edge. The water was dark and still. "There I am! If I see me, then you can see you."

The beaver pushed back his cap and bent over the side of the ferry to take a look. "I do see me. What do you know? It's time to go."

Two other beavers grabbed oars. They rowed the ferry across the lake.

Once on the other side, Kimani and Sasha galloped off into a large field. Flowers blazed with electric color. Big trees stood at the end of the field. Verdant Valley was beyond the big trees. Kimani ran faster.

"Wait a minute," Sasha called to her friend. "I'm hungry. Let's stop for a nibble."

She leaned over to take a bite of a delicious fuschia lily.

"Whoa!" She reared back.

Tiny letters were sprinkled like raindrops all over the petals.

Sasha blinked, shook her head, and moved closer to look at the lily.

They weren't just letters. They were words. And they were on all the flowers as far as Sasha could see.

How strange! Sasha thought.

Her eyes darted from word to word:

hero . . . bridge . . . snuffles. . . troll . . . sister . . . dollop . . .fire . . .

She blew on the flowers. The words rose from the petals and swirled in the air. They danced, moving in and out, and formed sentences with no meaning.

Troll sister snuffles bridge fire dollop hero.

Fire snuffles sister hero dollop troll bridge.

Sasha had never seen words on flowers before. Who had put them there?

Then Sasha heard a soft moan. She raised her ears and listened closely.

Another moan. Then a small burp. Then a sob.

"Hey, I hear crying," Sasha told Kimani.

"It's coming from there." Kimani pointed to a daisy. Its petals were closed, even though the sun was shining.

Sasha used her teeth to gently peel back the petals one by one.

"Oh, it's you!" she cried.

CHAPTER

7 Charmed

Collie sat cross-legged in the center of the daisy. Tiny tears streamed down her cheeks.

"What's wrong?" asked Kimani.

"I have a bellyache," sobbed Collie.

"I had one too. Do you want some lavender honey? It'll help." Sasha reached into her backpack for the pot. She dipped a spoon into it and held it out to Collie.

Collie opened her tiny mouth—and words spilled out!

Not words spoken out loud. Letters floated in the breeze. Words swirled and landed on nearby flowers.

"Collie! What's going on?" cried Sasha.

Collie clapped her hands over her mouth. She shook her head. She didn't want to tell them.

horse . . . sun . . . flying . . . dragon . . .

Sasha recognized these words!

"Collie! Are those words from the fabric? Are they from the history of the flying horses?" cried Sasha.

Collie nodded silently.

Sasha unrolled the blank fabric to show her. "Did you do this?"

Collie sobbed louder.

"It's okay," said Kimani. "Tell us what happened."

"No, Kimani. It's *not* okay," cried Sasha.

Kimani shot Sasha a warning look. "You can tell us, Collie. Really."

Sasha softened her voice. "Yes. Tell us, please."

"I didn't mean for this to happen, I promise. I loved those stories," whispered Collie.

"What happened?" Sasha tried to stay calm.

"You both fell asleep. I wanted to know more of the stories, but I can't read your language. I didn't want to wait until morning," explained Collie.

"So what did you do?" asked Kimani.

"I spoke a magical charm to have the stories read aloud to me, but it backfired. Somehow the stories ended up inside of me."

"Inside you?" cried Sasha. "How is that possible? You're so tiny and there are so many words!"

"Tell me about it. That's why my belly hurts so bad." Collie clutched her stomach. Then she let out a loud burp. Words spilled from her mouth: *music* . . . *rhubarb* . . . *jelly* . . . *star* . . .

"I'm so sorry!"

Sasha squeezed her eyes shut to think. The swirling words made her dizzy. "Let's see. You chanted a charm, but that charm didn't work. What if you chanted a different charm? A charm to reverse the first charm?"

"Yes! A charm to get the words out of you and back onto the fabric," said Kimani.

"I can try," agreed Collie. "I'm not very good at charms, though. Most plant pixies aren't."

"Something you should've thought of last night," Kimani pointed out.

"True." Collie groaned again and held her belly. Then she climbed up Sasha's snout and stood between her friend's ears for a better view of the fabric. She waved her hands in a circle.

"A spell was cast, now make it past.

"Words in me fly free.

"Back to the book, return what I once took."

They all waited. Would the charm work?

Pickle
pancake
diamond

CHAPTER 8

Caleb's Story

Sasha crossed her eyes. She looked up at Collie. She looked down at the fabric.

The fabric stayed blank. The stories stayed inside Collie. The reversal charm hadn't worked.

"I have a new idea. Try a really big jump," suggested Kimani.

"Okay . . ." Collie jumped. Words popped out of her mouth. She tried to catch as many as she could in her hands.

"We've got *diamond*, *pancake*, and *pickle*," Kimani cried.

"The words don't make sense out of order. They need to be in sentences. We can't read the stories this way," said Sasha.

"What are we going to do to get them back?" sobbed Collie.

"You're coming with us. Hang on tight to my mane." Sasha tucked the fabric into her backpack. She galloped toward the big trees. Soon they made it through the tangle of trees and entered Verdant Valley.

Sasha wanted to run right to her family's cottonwood tree and hug her mother, father, and sisters, but she had to find Caleb first.

She hurried toward the large pine tree where Caleb taught school. She spotted him getting ready for his lessons. He wrote letters in the dirt with his hoof.

"Sasha!" he cried, when she galloped up. "What's wrong?"

Sasha began to explain the disappearing history but was interrupted by Collie burping up a few words.

"The history of the flying horses has been erased. Can you get it back?" asked Sasha.

Caleb was silent. His old, watery eyes stared at the ground for so long that Sasha feared he'd fallen asleep. "All right then. I have a story for you," he said finally.

"We don't want a new story. We need to get Sapphire's stories back," said Sasha. "You don't understand."

"Listen and you'll understand." Caleb began his story. "Long ago, a herd of horses lived high in the mountains. Every winter, many froze in the bitter cold and got sick. One day a horse named Haydu told the herd he was leaving to join a group of elk. The horses were angry. Horses and elk don't like one another. They called him horrible names, and Haydu walked off. Winter raged on.

The horses huddled together in the icy winds. Then one day Haydu came back, pushing his way through the knee-high snow. He told the herd he'd joined the elk to find out where they went to escape from the winter. He showed the herd the path that the elk took around and down the mountain. At the bottom was a beautiful valley protected from the icy winds. Haydu had found the herd a new home. He'd been loyal to them all along."

"Haydu saved the horses," said Kimani.

"Haydu was my great-grandfather," said Caleb. "The valley he brought the herd to is Verdant Valley, where Sasha and I both grew up."

"Wow!" Sasha's eyes grew wide. "I never knew that."

"I have many stories about my ancestors," said Caleb. "They were told to me by my parents and my grandparents. They have not been written down. Instead, they are inside me."

"Like the flying horses' stories are inside Collie?" asked Kimani.

"Not the same way," said Caleb. "That's why Sapphire wants Sasha to learn the stories of the flying horses. Once they are inside you, the stories can never be erased. Sasha is an important link in the chain. She will tell the stories to the next generation of flying horses and they will tell the following generation."

"But the stories are all gone now," said Sasha.

"No, only the written words are gone. The stories are still out there, safe inside the horses who have heard them," said Caleb.

"Is there any way to get the words back on the fabric?" asked Sasha.

"You need powerful magic," said Caleb. "You need Sapphire."

CHAPTER 9

Powerful Magic Gum

Sasha, Kimani, and Collie flew back to Crystal Cove.

The winged horses were gathered around a large bonfire on the beach. The History Day celebrations had begun.

"Sasha!" the horses called. "We've been waiting for you. Please tell us a story."

"Yes, well, about that . . ." Sasha searched the crowd until she spotted Sapphire. She wished she could speak with her privately. "I'm thinking maybe later."

"Ho ho, princess. It's your turn now." Sapphire spoke calmly but firmly. "Go on. Let's hear the story you chose!"

The horses cheered for her. Sasha didn't have a choice. She stepped onto the stage. She slipped off her backpack and cleared her throat.

"Don't you need to read from the fabric?" asked Crimson.

Sasha reluctantly pulled out the rolled-up fabric. She placed it on a podium in front of her. Collie sat cross-legged on the podium with her back to the audience. She held her belly.

Should I open it? Sasha wondered. If she did, everyone would see it was blank.

"Actually, I don't need it," she said and kept the scroll closed. Sasha began to tell the story of a small, royal horse named Valentina who used spiders to stop Volcano, the fire-breathing dragon. Sasha was surprised the story was so easy to remember.

As Sasha spoke, the strangest thing happened. Words started flying out of Collie's mouth! They weren't random words like before. They were the sentences Sasha was saying, the words strung together in perfect order.

Sasha unrolled the fabric, and the words landed in the right places. Fascinated by the story, no one in the audience saw what was happening.

The horses stomped and neighed when Sasha finished. “More stories!” they chanted.

Oh, no! thought Sasha. *That's the only story I know. What should I do?*

Then she remembered what Caleb had told her.

"Wave your tail if you know a story from the history of the flying horses," she called to the crowd.

Several tails shot into the air.

Sasha called on the horses, one by one. They spoke of fierce battles, acts of kindness, and forever friendships. The flying horses told tales until the moon was full, and the fire had faded.

"Look!" cried Kimani, after the horses had gone to eat dinner in the meadow. "All the stories returned."

Each story the horses had told had spilled out of Collie and back onto the fabric.

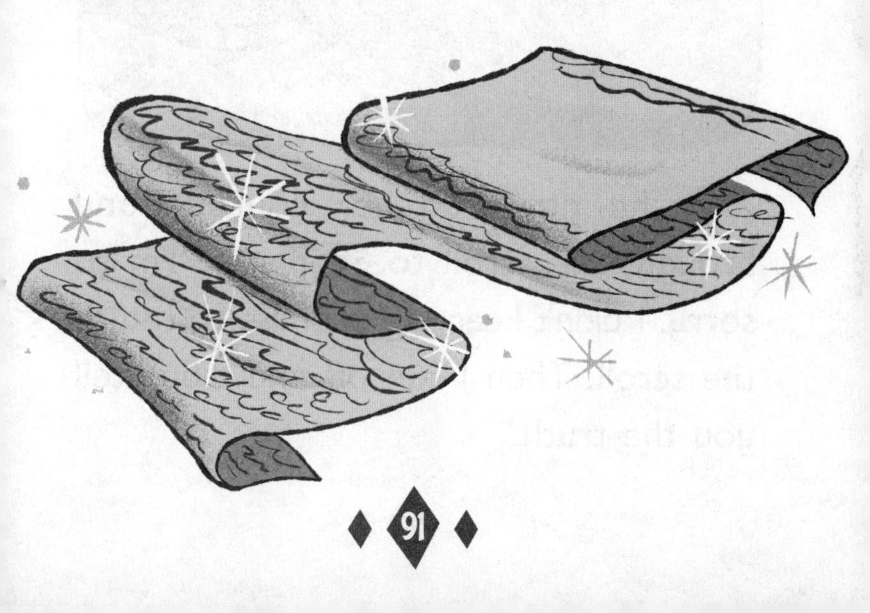

"Almost all of them." Sasha pointed down at the fabric. Several blank spaces still waited for stories that hadn't been told that night.

Sasha gathered her courage and brought the scroll to Sapphire. "I'm so sorry. I didn't keep my promise to return the scroll. Then I ran off and didn't tell you the truth."

Sapphire nodded. She'd known this already, but she was glad Sasha had finally told her. She gave Collie a large square of pink chewing gum. "Here, chew this."

Collie chomped on the gum and her tiny cheeks bulged. The words attached themselves to the wad of gum.

"Now blow the biggest bubble you can," instructed Sapphire.

Collie blew and blew. The sticky pink bubble grew and grew. It grew five times larger than the plant pixie!

Pop!

The bubble exploded and words flew from the gum and stuck onto the empty spaces of the fabric. Every word was back—and in the right order.

Sasha blinked. "Wow! That's powerful magic gum!"

"I had to counter my powerful magic," said Sapphire. "You see, I'm the one who made Collie's charm go bad."

"You?"

"I knew you didn't fully understand how important it is to really know our family stories," said Sapphire. "So I decided to teach you a little lesson."

"Little? You really scared me!" cried Sasha. "But I get it now. I see how important it is to know the stories and to have them inside me. That way I'll never lose them."

"Exactly!" Sapphire grinned and reached for the fabric. "I'll return this to the library. You can go eat dinner. You must be hungry after your journey."

"No," said Sasha. "The moon is full and bright and perfect for reading. I'm not hungry for wildflowers, I'm hungry for stories." Sasha smiled. "I have a lot of history to digest."

"Me, too!" Collie snuggled close to Sasha, eager to hear her royal friend read of the adventures of the magnificent flying horses. "Let's eat!"

Read on for a sneak peek from the tenth book in the Tales of Sasha series!

#10

Tales of SASHA

A Mystery Message

by Alexa Pearl

illustrated by Paco Sordo

CHAPTER

1 Up in the Air

"Follow me!" Wyatt called to Sasha.

Wyatt galloped across the field. It had rained for days, but the sun had come out this afternoon. Raindrops still sparkled on the emerald-green grass.

"Do everything I do," said Wyatt.

"I will, but I'll do it better!" Sasha galloped behind him.

Wyatt made a sharp turn. Sasha made a sharp turn.

He ran in a zigzag. She ran in a zigzag.

Wyatt jumped over a log. Sasha jumped over a log.

Her best friend ran fast. Sasha ran fast, too.

Then she looked up. Oh, no! They were racing toward a humongous rock that towered over them.

Is he going to jump over it? she wondered. The rock was so tall!

Wyatt ran toward it. Faster and faster.

Sasha opened her mouth to cry out when—

Wyatt leaped!

Sasha held her breath.

Wyatt made it over safely.

Sasha breathed out—but then the rock was in front of *her*. She wasn't ready to jump. She was about to crash!

She had only one choice. Her wings opened wide, and she rose into the air, soaring above the rock. A moment later, her hooves hit the ground.

Wyatt whirled around. "Hey, no fair! You cheated."

"Me? No way," said Sasha. "I *don't* cheat."

"Flying is cheating," said Wyatt.

"Since when?" asked Sasha.

"Since you can fly and I can't," said Wyatt. "You have to stay on the ground for this game. Otherwise, it's totally unfair."

Sasha was a flying horse with beautiful wings that had sparkly feathers and had only just found out she could fly. Nothing was more fun than flying. But her best friend Wyatt didn't have wings.

"Cross my wings, I'll play fair," Sasha promised. "Even without flying, I can do anything you can."

"Let's see!" Wyatt ducked under a low tree branch. Sasha ducked under the branch, too. He took four steps backward.

"Tricky!" cried Sasha. She walked backward, too.

Wyatt galloped quickly across the meadow.

The white patch on the center of Sasha's back began to itch. She kept galloping. The itching grew stronger. She knew exactly what the itching meant. It meant her body wanted to fly!

No, thought Sasha. She'd promised Wyatt she wouldn't use her wings.

She closed her eyes, trying to make the feeling pass. *No flying, no flying*, she chanted to herself.

Slowly . . . slowly . . . the itchiness faded.

"Sasha! You're cheating again!"

Sasha's eyes snapped open at the sound of Wyatt's voice. She twisted her head to the right and to the left, searching for her friend.

"Down here!" Wyatt called from the ground below.

Sasha was up in the sky—and she was flying! She hadn't flapped her wings or taken off. What was happening?